ONCE UPON A
DECEMBER

A Holiday
Short Story
Collection

Sydney Logan

Summaries

What Child Is This?

Estranged from his family and the love of his life, Thomas Fisher finds himself stranded in an airport on Christmas Eve. Imagine his surprise when a young boy takes him by the hand and shows him the way home.

Mistletoe Magic

Melanie Taylor is on a mission to find the perfect Christmas gift for her husband. Something special. Something expensive. Something that will save her marriage. Can a chance encounter on an elevator make her Christmas wish come true?

The Little Drummer Boy

It's Christmas Eve, and Justin Banks is on the hunt for a last-minute gift for his wife, Megan. With the help of a homeless man and the beat of a drum, Justin stumbles upon the one thing Megan has always wanted. The one thing money can't buy. It's amazing what we can hear if we just take a moment and really listen.

Table of Contents

Acknowledgments

Christmas short stories have become a holiday tradition for me. With this new story, I decided to combine it with my two previously published shorts and offer it in both digital and print format. I know some readers, like my mom, prefer to hold a book in their hands. This is for you.

Thank you to my dream team of editors, Wendy Depperschmidt, Shaina Hanson, and Kathie Spitz. They've edited every word I've ever published, and I am beyond grateful for their hard work and for their friendship.

To T.M. Franklin, who took time away from promoting her new book to make the beautiful cover for this collection. Thank you for being my friend.

To the ladies of Author to Author for helping promote, offering advice, and being voices of reason. Special thanks to Sandi Layne for the applesauce.

To Jessica and Chasity, my publicists at Rock Star PR, for being fun and professional! I appreciate all you do for me.

Thank you to Lindsey Gray for her book formatting services.

To JA Hensley for making my beautiful book swag and, most importantly, for always being there for me.

Special thanks to Sydney's Sweethearts on Facebook. All the posts and Tweets make such a difference. Thank you for loving my stories.

To my husband, who encourages me even though sci-fi is really his thing. I love you.

To the bloggers who continue to read, review, and promote my books. Thank you for your support!

Finally, thank you to my readers. I hope these Christmas stories put you in the holiday spirit.

What Child Is This?

The airport's full of aggravated travelers, desperate to make it home for Christmas. Thanks to an unexpected snow storm out west, flights in and out of Atlanta have come to a virtual standstill. The monitors flash with cancellations and delays, and with each new screen update, a symphony of groans can be heard throughout the gate area. Behind the counter, equally frustrated ticket agents attempt to please the stranded passengers.

I've seen it all. Tears. Screams. Tantrums.

And that's just from the adults.

As for me? I'm just trying to get to a business meeting.

"Sir," the agent says to the passenger in front of me, "we're doing everything we can to get you—"

"You're not doing enough!" The frazzled man points toward his family standing off to the side. "You explain to my kids why they aren't going to make it to Grandma's house for Christmas!"

The woman apologizes again and offers him a hotel for the night. The angry man stalks away to consult with his wife. Shaking my head, I step up to the counter and offer the agent my ticket.

"Good evening, Mr. Fisher. I'm sorry for the inconvenience."

It *is* an inconvenience, but I force a smile anyway. The last thing this woman needs is another irate passenger.

"It's not your fault. You can't control the weather."

She sighs with relief. "Thank you for understanding. Let's see what we can do to get you to New York as soon as possible."

"I appreciate that."

While she works her magic, I pull my phone out of my jacket and scroll through about a hundred unread emails. Unlike the rest of the travelers, I'm not desperate to get anywhere to celebrate the holiday. However, two days

1

after Christmas, I'm scheduled to meet the owner of a stagnant, yet potentially profitable, software company. December means one thing to me— significant end-of-year profits. In our crappy economy, it also means the end of the line for many struggling corporations. That's when I get to work my own kind of holiday magic. I swoop in, buy the drowning business for mere pennies, and then sell it for a substantial return.

Needless to say, *Sullivan Software* is just one of the many companies on Thomas Fisher's Christmas list.

"Mr. Fisher, I have good news. There's a short delay, but your flight should be boarding soon."

Happy to be the bearer of good news for at least one person in her line, the agent smiles brightly and hands me my boarding pass. I thank her and try to ignore the jealous stares of the rest of the travelers as I make my way to a seat. I spend the next forty minutes answering emails, deleting others, and confirming my hotel reservation in Manhattan. My secretary would typically handle this stuff, but in the spirit of the season, I'd given her two weeks off, with pay. I may have the reputation of Scrooge, but I understand that some people actually enjoy spending time with their family during the holidays.

I'm not one of those people.

It's not that I don't love them. That's the problem. I love them too much.

I love *her* too much.

My flight's called, and I grab my bag and board the plane. After stuffing my carry-on in the compartment, I fasten my seatbelt and pretend to listen as the flight attendant gives her safety spiel. I check my phone one last time and notice a text from my sister, Shaina.

Please come home for Christmas this year?

I don't bother replying. She knows I'm not coming home. I just power off my phone and stuff it back into my jacket. With a tired sigh, I lean back, close my eyes, and find myself doing the one thing I try never to do.

I think about the mess I've made of my life.

Ten years ago, I'd been an eighteen-year-old living in Paisley Springs, Tennessee—a tiny, rural town about two hours north of Nashville. Ten years ago, I'd been a popular athlete with dreams of becoming a professional basketball player. Ten years ago, I'd been the golden child of Dr. Benjamin and Olivia Fisher.

Ten years ago, I'd been a boy in love.

I still am.

Life is full of highways, and some are just too long when you're trying to find your way home. In my case, some forgotten roads completely disappear. Time erases them, to the point that you begin to wonder if they ever really existed in the first place.

But they did. I know they did.

I close my eyes and try to ignore the image that flickers behind my eyelids. In my mind, Emma Hayes is still eighteen years old. With her long red hair and deep green eyes, she'd always looked at me as if I was her dream come true.

And I was, until I ripped those dreams away.

We were together for more than a year, and it had been the happiest time of my life. But being crazy in love makes you do stupid things. Careless things.

And then things happen that you never imagined would happen to you.

When Emma told me she was pregnant, I questioned if the baby was even mine. The accusation was ridiculous, considering I'd been her first and she'd been mine, and we'd been inseparable since our first date. When her dad showed up at my house, he and his rifle made it clear that I was expected to take care of my responsibilities.

There'd been no question in my mind that I loved her. Emma was smart, funny, and everything I could have ever wanted in a girlfriend . . . and someday, in a wife. I'd never been a romantic person or believed in love at first sight, but Emma Hayes had made a believer out of me.

Then I ruined it all by being the biggest jerk imaginable.

During the third month of her pregnancy, when her morning sickness was at its worst, the enormity of our situation began to weigh heavily on me. When our parents told me I'd have to find a full-time job and forego college to take care of my new family, I became bitter. And with that bitterness, I said a lot of things I shouldn't have. Hurtful words I didn't mean. Hateful words that made her cry. Heartbreaking words that sent Emma to the hospital, where she miscarried.

My fault.

The doctor told me I wasn't to blame, but I didn't believe him. I could tell by the look in Emma's eyes that she didn't believe him, either. Her green eyes, once so bright with love for me, were now hard and cold. And my parents, who used to be so proud of me, now looked at me like I was a monster. *Because I was.*

We graduated high school a month later, and I packed everything I could fit into my car and fled to the nearest community college. I worked full-time while going to school and eventually transferred to Belmont to complete my degree in finance. After that, I moved to Atlanta and spent six months working as an intern for an investment group before being offered a salaried position in the Mergers and Acquisitions division of the company.

While I'm a professional success, I'm a complete failure when it comes to my personal life.

I haven't been home in ten years. I won't even fly through the state of Tennessee if I can avoid it. Some days, like today, it's unavoidable. Out of obligation to my mother, I check in with my family from time-to-time, but it's a brief Skype call. They never mention Emma and I never ask. No matter what she's doing now, and no matter who she's with, I know she's better off without me. As for me, I haven't even tried to fall in love.

It's impossible to love again when every face I see is hers.

"Sir?" My eyes snap open to find a flight attendant standing over me. "I'll need you to fasten your seatbelt before landing."

I blink rapidly. We can't possibly be in New York already.

"Landing?"

"Yes, sir. Weather conditions have become unfavorable, so we're having to divert to Nashville."

"Nashville?"

"Yes. Hopefully it won't be too long of a delay. But in the meantime, welcome to Tennessee."

I almost laugh. *Can the universe really be that cruel?*

Yes. Yes, it can.

The furious voices of holiday travelers echo in the air of Nashville International Airport. An angry mob's already formed at the ticket counter, screaming at the bewildered ticket agents, but it's obvious to anyone that can read a weather map that no flights will be departing from Nashville anytime soon. The storm that dumped two feet of snow in Kansas is making its way east. Unfortunately, it hit the Volunteer State in the form of ice.

Ice is bad.

It's all turned to snow now, and while that's not much better, at least there's some traction there. Neither type of precipitation is conducive to me getting out of this state anytime soon.

I'm not at all surprised when the ticket agents report that, unless we'd like to stay in a hotel, we might as well find a spot and make ourselves comfortable for the night. As I drop into the nearest seat, I can't help but laugh. I'm stranded, in the one place in the world I *really* don't want to be stranded.

Merry Christmas to me.

"You're two hours away from your family in Paisley Springs. Don't you think you should at least call them?"

I turn my head toward the voice, and I'm startled to find myself staring into a set of bright green eyes. He's just a kid, dressed in a red hoodie and jeans and playing some kind of game on his iPad. His hair's dark, and I can't help but notice it's nearly the same shade as mine . . . and just as unruly. I'm about to tell the kid he might as well embrace it, because there isn't a hair product on the market that will tame it, but then I realize he mentioned my family.

"Excuse me? What did you say?"

"Your family. You know . . . your mom and dad? Your sister?"

"What about them?"

"They miss you."

"And how the hell would you know that?"

He grimaces, probably because I cursed. I don't know much about kids, but he looks old enough to have said a few cuss words in his short little life. I bet that video game is just full of them.

"Because I know."

The kid shrugs and turns his attention back to his game.

Annoyed, and just a little freaked out, I grab my bag and head to the restroom. I quickly splash cold water on my face and try to get my blood pressure under control. *Who is this kid? How does he know my family? And how does he know I'm two hours away from home?* I close my eyes and try to regulate my breathing, only to have to start the entire process over again when I open them to find the kid sitting on the sink . . . and still staring down at his game.

"Are you following me now?"

"You're very rude."

"And you're a pain in the ass. Why are you bothering me? Where are your parents?"

The boy slowly lowers his iPad and levels me with a steely look that knocks the breath out of me. His eyes are so green. Almost as green as—

"She misses you, too."

Okay, this is officially weird.

"Who misses me?"

The boy rolls his eyes.

"*She* does."

For just a moment, I allow myself to believe it.

"No, she doesn't. She's better off without me. They're all better off."

"You're wrong."

Once again, I'm fascinated by the lost look in his eyes. The resemblance is heartbreakingly remarkable.

I shake my head. "Well, kid, this has been loads of fun, but why don't I help you find your parents?"

He smiles sadly at me.

"I think you need to see," he says, jumping off the counter. "And I think I need to be the one to show you. Why don't you rent a car or call us a cab or something?"

I laugh and grab my bag. "I'm not going anywhere, and neither are you. Not with me, anyway."

"Why not?"

Sighing tiredly, I head out of the restroom and back into the insanity of the airport. Families have begun to build makeshift campsites on the floor. I collapse into the nearest empty chair and scroll through my phone, searching for the nearest hotel.

Of course he follows me.

"The car rental place is on the other side of the airport," he says.

"Look, kid, I don't know if anyone's told you, but there's an ice storm coming. I'm not renting a car and driving to Paisley Springs tonight. And even if I did, you wouldn't be going with me."

"Why not?"

"Because I'd be charged with kidnapping?"

"Nah, it's cool. And the highway to Paisley Springs is clear."

"And how do you know that?"

"Because I have an app that says so. See?"

He hands me the iPad, and sure enough, there's an app on the screen displaying road conditions throughout the state. According to it, the highway to Paisley Springs is clear. For now, anyway.

"Seems kind of stupid to stay in a hotel when your family's so close," he says.

"You don't understand."

"I understand you're chicken shit."

I smirk. *So he does curse.*

"Nice language, kid."

He grins.

"Thanks. I get it from my dad."

❋❋❋

I have no idea what possesses me to listen to him. No idea at all why I'm now driving toward Paisley Springs with this kid in the passenger seat.

"Are you sure you don't need to call your parents or something?"

"Nope. It's cool."

Do parents really let their kids loose like this? I have no idea.

"Okay . . . so what's your name?"

I figure if I'm going to prison for kidnapping, I might as well know the name of the kid who put me there.

"Xander. It's *Alexander.* I just like Xander better."

Huh.

"Weird. My middle name is Alexander."

"Huh."

Officially crazy.

"I'm Thomas Fisher."

"I know."

Of course he knows.

"How old are you, Xander?"

"You sure ask a lot of questions."

"Yeah, well, I'm hoping I'll bore you to death and you'll fall asleep. Then I can just keep on driving."

"You don't want to see your family?"

"It's complicated."

"That's not a *no.*"

I mutter a curse under my breath.

"And you can keep driving, but we'll end up in Kentucky. The roads aren't so clear up there."

I groan with annoyance and tell him to play his game.

Snow begins to fall as we get closer to Paisley Springs. Thankfully, the roads are still clear—of both ice and drivers, which makes the trip much easier. The two hours fly, and before I even realize it, we're parked in front of my parents' house.

"It's been ten years since I've seen this place," I murmur.

Christmas lights shine brightly from the front porch, and a gigantic gold and green wreath hangs proudly on the front door. Mom always loved decorating for the holidays. It seems a little minimal this year, but they're older now. I try not to think about that too much.

"I can't go inside."

Xander nods. "Maybe just peek through the window?"

I can do that. I can just peek.

It's a slippery walk up the sidewalk. Of course, Xander's right on my heels, talking nonstop and driving me nuts. *Doesn't he realize how nervous I am?*

"You're just peeking," the little mind reader says. "Don't be nervous."

We walk around the side of the house to the living room window. Taking a deep breath, I peek inside. A brilliantly decorated Christmas tree stands in the corner with only a few presents nestled below its branches. Like always, our stockings hang from the mantle of the fireplace, and above them, Mom's Christmas village is displayed. I smile when I see the little train making its circuit around the miniature town. When I was a kid, I could watch that train for hours.

Suddenly, my family appears in the living room, holding small bowls. Mom and Dad sit down on the couch while my sister finds a spot next to the tree. I catch a glimpse of the pattern on the tiny bowls, and my heart leaps in my chest.

"Applesauce," Xander says.

My eyes flash to him. "How do you know that?"

"I can smell it. It's my favorite food."

"It's my favorite food, too, but you can't *smell* it from here."

"Sure you can. Try."

I roll my eyes but decide to humor the kid. Closing my eyes, I inhale deeply, and instantly, I'm ten years old again.

"Cinnamon!" I whisper excitedly.

Xander just smiles.

"Homemade applesauce was always a Christmas tradition," I explain quietly. "It's an old recipe of my grandmother's, and when I was little, I used to sit on the counter and watch as Mom chopped up the apples. When I got older, she let me help. Every Christmas Eve, we would sit around the tree and eat our applesauce before we opened gifts."

"You opened gifts on Christmas Eve?" Xander asked.

I smile as memories flood me. My first bike. My leather jacket. The keys to my first car.

"Yeah, but there were always more presents to open in the morning. Those gifts were from Santa."

Xander says nothing as I look through the window once more. Of course, my parents look older, but it's not their age that depresses me the most.

"They look so sad. I wonder why that is?" I ask, not really expecting an answer.

"Because they miss you," Xander replies simply, as if this is obvious. "You're their only son, and your mom decorates every year and makes homemade applesauce, hoping that this year will be the Christmas you come home."

"She makes it every year?"

"Every year."

My mom places her bowl on the coffee table and walks over to the Christmas tree. I hold my breath as she lightly traces her fingers along one of the ornaments. It's red and gold, and I know without a doubt that it's the ornament with my name on it. I'd made it in Sunday school class when I was eight years old.

"She hangs it every year. Just hoping . . ."

It's too much. Too many memories and too much shame.

I close my eyes and lean back against the cold brick of the house.

Seeing my family so sad is complete torture. I thought they'd be happy that I'd stayed away all this time. I'd embarrassed them . . . shamed them. And I'd gone out of my way to avoid them for the past decade. *How can they possibly still love me?*

"They love you because you're their son," Xander says. "They say the bond between a parent and child is nearly impossible to break, even in death. Do you really think a few thousand miles is going to change how they feel about you?"

With wide eyes, I stare at this kid.

"How did you get so smart?"

He just grins.

"I get it from my mom."

"This is a bad idea," I mutter as we drive down Main Street.

Paisley Springs looks just the same, except for a few new restaurants. When we were kids, Emma and I used to call it Mayberry, from the *Andy Griffith Show*. At the time, it wasn't a flattering comment, but now that I'm older, I can appreciate the tranquility of my little hometown.

Maybe Mayberry isn't so bad, after all.

"This is the best idea ever," Xander says, bouncing in his seat. "You know you want to see her."

"Of course, I want to see her."

That's when I realize I have no idea where to find her. *Does she even live in Paisley Springs?*

"She works at the diner," Xander says.

"The Paisley Diner? She's still there?"

Xander nods, and in that moment, I feel a knife twist in my gut. If Emma's still working at the diner, that probably means she didn't go to college. She always wanted to be a lawyer. *Why didn't she go to law school?*

"Her high school GPA was crap," Xander explains, reading my mind once again.

"No, it wasn't. She had a 4.0 before . . . before . . ."

Before she miscarried.

"She didn't have a 4.0 . . . *after*," he says.

I don't bother asking how he knows that. I stopped asking questions right after I smelled the applesauce.

Emma's still living in Paisley Springs and working at the diner—the same place she'd worked back in high school. Has she never worked anywhere else? Did her grades really suffer that much? And if so, how did I not know that? Had I honestly been so wrapped up in my own adolescent selfishness that I didn't realize how much losing the baby affected *her*?

I feel like such a fool. I've spent the last ten years avoiding everyone I love, thinking that's what they needed in order to move on with their lives. But in reality, for all of them, time has stood still.

Have they all been waiting for me?

We reach the diner, and I park the car. Xander takes my trembling hand in his as he leads me up the gravel path and toward the entrance. The place looks relatively vacant, which isn't too surprising since it's late on Christmas Eve.

"Are we peeking again?" Xander asks.

"Yes."

He sighs and pulls me toward the window. The diner really is empty except for a few coffee drinkers sitting at the counter.

"She could have gone to community college," I whisper into the air. "Did she even try?"

"Nope. She was waiting for you to come back. You'd made plans."

We had made plans. We'd planned to move away from Paisley Springs and attend college . . . together.

I forced myself to move on without her . . . to live without her, and all this time she's been waiting for me?

Just then, a waitress appears from the back. She's holding a coffee pot and smiling at the customers. Her long red hair is pulled into a ponytail. And her eyes . . . her green eyes are still the most beautiful eyes in the world.

Xander's hand tightens around mine.

"She prays for you every night," he says as we watch her pour coffee into a man's mug. "She prays that you'll come home, but if you don't, she hopes that you're at least happy."

Emma wasted her prayers on me. I haven't been happy in more than ten years.

"And she never loved another soul."

Neither have I.

"She must hate me," I whisper, the agony so intense that I think I might collapse under the weight of it. Xander just holds my hand a little tighter.

"She still loves you. She'll forgive you."

"She doesn't look *unhappy*."

But even as the words slip out of my mouth, I know it's a lie. Even now, I know every curve of her smile and every sparkle in her eye, and I can tell she's faking it.

"It's almost closing time," Xander says. "You can't walk through locked doors, so I suggest you get inside."

I look away from the beautiful angel standing behind the glass and down into the eyes of this crazy, green-eyed boy.

"You'll come with me?"

He smiles brightly.

"Don't you understand? I'm already there."

I don't understand, and I tell him so.

"Don't you see? I've watched over both of you for the past ten years. She prays for you every night and you think about her a thousand times a day. You're still crazy about each other. I just wanted to see you guys together."

"I . . . don't understand."

The child's bright green eyes meet mine. "My name is Alexander, and I love homemade applesauce. I have my dad's crazy hair and my mom's green eyes, and all I want for Christmas is for my mom and dad to be happy."

A tear trickles down my face.

It all makes sense now.

Is he an angel? A ghost? A figment of my heartbroken imagination?

It doesn't matter, because behind the glass, his mom is waiting for me.

But first thing's first . . .

I kneel on the ground and place my hands on each side of his face. He really is a beautiful child. The spitting image of her. And of me.

"I've always loved your mother. And *you*. I didn't know it then, but I do now. Never doubt that."

My son smiles. "I don't doubt it. We love you, too."

I lean close and kiss his forehead.

"By the way, you should know that Mom isn't able to have children. She never was."

"Never?"

"The doctors said never. It wasn't your fault."

I wrap my arms around my son and pull him close, hugging him tightly.

"Mom's waiting," he whispers.

With a nod, I climb to my feet.

"Are you leaving?"

"No." Xander smiles and points toward the window. "I'm peeking."

I smile through my tears. "Will I ever see you again?"

"You'll see me every day."

"But how?"

"Anytime you feel like you're missing me, you just have to look into her green eyes. I'm there. I think her eyes will be brighter now. Oh! Wait a sec . . ."

Xander pulls a piece of mistletoe out of his pocket and hands it to me. I don't even bother asking where it came from. Nothing makes sense tonight, but maybe it's not supposed to.

"Use this. You know, in case you need motivation to kiss her."

"I don't think that'll be a problem." I chuckle and kiss his forehead one last time. "Thank you, Xander."

He pushes me toward the door, and I take a deep breath before reaching for the handle. As I walk inside the diner, I take comfort in knowing that my son's standing just outside the window . . .

Peeking.

The diner's completely deserted now, so I gently turn the closed sign on the door before making my way to the counter. I sit down on a stool and wait. My entire body trembles with anticipation, and I'm pretty sure I'm going to pass out just as Emma walks through the swinging doors, holding a bowl.

"Sorry, we're—"

She stops talking.

I stop breathing.

Emma blinks a few times, looks down into her bowl, and then up at me again. She's probably trying to decide if she's finally lost her mind.

I can relate.

"Thomas?"

"It's me."

Suddenly, she smiles the most beautiful smile I've ever seen.

"Xander sent you?"

"More like . . . dragged me, but yeah."

Emma laughs, and with that sound, every ounce of tension leaves my body.

"He told me he would. I didn't believe him."

Emma places the bowl in front of me on the counter. I don't even look down. I can smell the cinnamon.

"You see him, too?"

She nods. I look behind my shoulder and through the glass, but I can't see him anymore.

"Will he come back?" I ask.

"I don't know. I never know. But I have to believe he will."

I reach over the counter and lift my hand, letting my fingers drift along her face. Tears spill down the softest cheeks I've ever touched.

"He will, if for no other reason than to make sure I'm not totally screwing this up again. That is, if you'll let me try to make it right."

With a nod, she smiles through her own tears, her green eyes shining brightly.

"I love you, Emma."

"I love you, too."

"Still?"

"Always."

I don't really need the mistletoe, but I pull it out of my pocket anyway . . . just in case he's peeking . . . and I hold it above our heads.

We lean in, and I slowly brush my lips against hers.

And with that kiss, I'm finally home.

Mistletoe Magic

Last-minute shopping on Christmas Eve always struck fear in Melanie Taylor's heart. The frantic customers. The exhausted cashiers. The long lines. All of it was mayhem, and the last thing she needed was more chaos in her life.

In an attempt to avoid the crowds, Melanie had chosen a high-end department store to do the last of her shopping. There was only one gift left on her list, and it had to be special. And in her world, special was just another word for *expensive*.

Melanie stood at a glass case, looking down at the selection of designer watches. The one that caught her eye was undeniably gorgeous, made of titanium ceramic, and equipped with enough functions to pilot a small plane.

"May I help you?" The man behind the counter beamed. It was impossible to ignore the excitement in his voice.

Melanie pointed at the silver watch. "I'd like to see that one, please."

"Oh, that's a fine choice," he said as he reached for his keys. The man lifted the watch out of the case and handed it to her. She didn't bother looking at the expensive price tag. Instead, she gazed at the band, and then at the watch's face, hoping either would trigger some recollection.

Nothing.

The man noticed her reluctance.

"Shopping for your husband?"

"Yes, I am."

"What a wonderful Christmas gift! Your husband would be proud to wear a watch so beautiful and well-crafted . . ."

The man continued his sales pitch, but it was easy to ignore. He had no way of knowing that the price of the watch wasn't the cause of Melanie's hesitation. It was the fact that, just last year, in this same department store, she had bought a watch for her husband for Christmas.

And she couldn't remember what it looked like.

A desperate Melanie glanced at the man behind the counter. He didn't look familiar, either, but that was hardly helpful. Still, she decided to ask.

"Were you working last Christmas Eve, as well?"

It was a long shot, she knew. But perhaps he remembered her, and if he did, maybe he could recall if she'd bought this exact watch.

The manager looked confused.

"No, ma'am. I just recently moved from . . . up north."

She smiled sheepishly. This nice man probably had a family and wished he could be with them on Christmas Eve instead of dealing with privileged customers like her—especially ones who couldn't recall if they had bought their spouse this same ten-thousand dollar watch just last year.

With a sigh, Melanie glanced down at her own watch. The store closed in twenty minutes.

"I'll take it," Melanie decided. "I just hope I have time to gift-wrap it."

The manager smiled brightly as she placed the platinum card in his hand. Of course, he was ecstatic. The commission from this sale would probably ensure that his family had a very merry Christmas.

"Do you have children?" Melanie asked.

The manager handed her the receipt to sign. "Yes, I do. Two girls. Both blondes, just like their beautiful mother."

The pride in his voice made Melanie smile as she scribbled her name on the slip.

"Well, I hope you, and they, have a lovely holiday . . ."

"Nick," the man said. "My name is Nick, and I wish you and your husband a Merry Christmas."

"Thank you, Nick. I wish for that, too."

He had no idea how much she wished for that.

Nick handed Melanie a pretty gift bag. It was red and silver, and festive enough that she wouldn't have to bother with gift wrapping at all.

Her mission complete, she took a few moments to browse through the rest of the store. At one of the counters, she overheard a man and his son, trying to decide between a leather handbag and a bottle of designer perfume for the mom. Unlike Melanie, the two of them had smiles on their faces. They were happy customers, excited to find something that would brighten the eyes of someone they loved.

Melanie, on the other hand, had just hoped to find something that would make her husband notice her, even if it was just for one day.

On her way to the elevator, Melanie couldn't help but think about the nice store manager and his wish for her. As much as she hoped for a wonderful Christmas with her husband, her only concern right now was that he didn't already own a watch just like the one in this bag.

And that was the prayer she whispered as she stepped onto the elevator.

The first thing Ethan noticed was her long legs. They were hidden beneath the fabric of her black dress and stylish overcoat, but they peeked out as she walked onto the elevator. Without acknowledging him, she pressed the button that would take her to the first floor.

Ethan's appreciative gaze swept over her. She was a beautiful woman, with long, dark hair that curled just slightly on the ends. For just a moment, he considered reaching out and letting his fingers touch the silky strands, but sanity prevailed, and he quickly stuffed his free hand in his pocket.

Instead, he cleared his throat and Melanie jumped, turning toward the sound. Her eyes widened when she saw him. He was dressed in a charcoal gray suit and light blue tie—a perfect complement to his soft eyes. One hand was in his pocket while the other held a small gift bag.

"Doing some last-minute shopping?" Ethan asked.

Melanie blinked rapidly before nodding.

"I am," she replied stiffly. "You?"

He lifted the gold bag, giving it a little shake.

She nodded. "For someone special?"

"For my wife. You?"

"My husb—"

Her reply was cut short when the lights dimmed, and the elevator lurched to a stop.

"Fantastic," Melanie mumbled.

The emergency lights flickered on, and Ethan pushed the alarm button before grabbing the elevator's phone. Melanie listened intently as he barked orders to someone before slamming down the receiver.

"The entire block is in the dark," Ethan grumbled. He removed his jacket before settling himself on the floor.

"What are you doing?"

"Getting comfortable," Ethan said. "The guy said it might be a while."

Melanie glanced down at her silk dress.

"I'm not sitting on this dirty floor."

Ethan shrugged. "Suit yourself."

Melanie eyed his jacket.

"Speaking of *suits*, isn't that Armani?"

"I have no idea which expensive name is stitched on the label."

She smirked. "But you know it's expensive."

"There isn't a suit in my closet that didn't cost a fortune. My wife insists upon it."

"Maybe that's because your wife has good taste."

"Maybe that's because my wife is too hung-up on labels." Ethan loosened his tie and sighed tiredly. "Just sit down. I hate enclosed spaces, and you're making me nervous."

A stubborn Melanie remained on her feet, but the four-inch heels of her favorite boots weren't the most comfortable, and after a few minutes, she finally relented and removed her coat. It was far less expensive than the dress, after all. She placed it on the floor before slowly sitting down.

"See? Isn't that better?"

Melanie sighed loudly.

"One of us should probably conserve our cell battery," Ethan suggested, pulling his phone out of his pocket. "My Blackberry has a full charge, so I don't mind keeping mine on if you'd like to save yours."

With a nod, Melanie reached into her bag and turned off her iPhone.

"You don't want to text someone first?" Ethan asked. "Your husband might worry if you come home late."

Melanie somehow resisted the urge to laugh.

"No one worries about me," she said.

A brief look passed between them before they both quickly looked away.

"What about you? You don't want to send a text to your label-loving wife to let her know you're stuck in an elevator?"

"No need."

"Why not?"

Ethan gazed impassively at the pretty brunette.

"Nobody worries about me, either," he replied.

Leaning her head back against the steel wall, Melanie took a deep breath and closed her eyes. After a few moments of suffocating silence, Ethan finally broke the ice.

"We didn't used to be this way," he said softly. "Once upon a time, my wife and I were crazy about one another. She laughed all the time, and her laughter was all it took to make me smile. We couldn't keep our hands off each other, and nothing was more important than making the other person happy."

Melanie opened her eyes and glanced over at the handsome man.

"That sounds nice."

"It was."

"What happened?"

It was the same question he asked himself every single day.

Ethan shrugged. "Life. Money. Heartbreak. At some point, *appearing* to have the perfect marriage became more important than actually having

18

one."

Melanie knew all about keeping up appearances. She and her husband attended social functions all the time. They held hands and smiled for the cameras, and everyone assumed their marriage was picture-perfect.

If they only knew . . .

"My wife buries her nose in a book or volunteers at the hospital while I camp out at the office. By the time I get home, she's asleep."

"Or she's faking it," Melanie whispered guiltily. How many nights had her husband walked into their bedroom, only to find her supposedly sleeping?

"Faking it? Why would she do that?"

"Maybe because when the two of you talk, it always ends in an argument."

Ethan sighed deeply and leaned his head back against the wall. It was true. All he and his wife had done was bicker for the past six months. He was hoping this Christmas could be a new start, and the last-minute gift in the bag was symbolic of that wish.

"I love my wife. She has no idea how much. We've been together ten years, and still, I've never met anyone so beautiful and so. . . *good*. She's kind and compassionate. Always the first to volunteer for anything. Especially for children's charities . . ."

His voice trailed off, and Melanie heard the sadness in his voice.

"Do you tell her?"

Ethan tilted his head. "Tell her what?"

"All the things you just told me."

He tried to recall how long it had been since he told his wife how much he loved her. They used to say it every day. Each morning. Each night. At the end of every phone call. How long *had* it been? Granted, it was hard to talk to a brick wall, and when the wall was asleep by the time he found the courage to drag himself home from work . . .

"No, I don't tell her." His voice was filled with shame.

"I bet she'd love to hear it."

Ethan noticed her wistful tone, and it made his heart ache.

"She probably would. You . . . sound as if you have some experience with this."

Melanie twirled the platinum band on her finger. It was a nervous habit that had come along within the past few months. Her psychiatrist found it interesting, spewing some nonsense about how Melanie obviously found a sense of peace in the diamond on her hand. That perhaps the ring served as a reminder of a happier time.

Melanie hated her shrink.

"Our situations are similar," she said quietly. "My husband isn't a bad man. We avoid each other like the plague, because that's what our marriage has become. We barely talk, and when we do, it always ends in a fight. We don't touch. Kiss. Hug."

Ethan nodded grimly. He didn't even bother to ask about sex. He knew. It was nonexistent.

"I love my husband. We've just . . . lost our way, I guess. And I don't know that we can ever get back on track."

"But you *were* happy?"

"At one time, yes."

Ethan sighed heavily and gazed at the woman.

"I was happy, too," he said. "I can still remember the first time I saw her. She was wearing a bulky college sweatshirt. Hair in a ponytail. Chewing on the end of her pen while listening intently to the professor. And all I could do was stare, because she was so pretty. She still is. She is still the most beautiful girl I've ever seen."

Melanie couldn't help but smile.

"I was taking a creative writing class, and he needed an easy elective," she said. "We fell hard, very quickly. He has this dimple in his chin that made every girl on campus swoon, but for some reason, he chose me. We got married as soon as we graduated. I started editing children's books, and he began working at his dad's law firm. Now, he's a partner. Someday, the entire company will belong to him, and I don't care. I never cared about the money or prestige. All I ever wanted was a happy marriage." She laughed, but there wasn't a trace of humor in her voice. "I just bought a ten-thousand dollar watch for my husband, and it's quite possibly the same watch I bought him last year. I can't even remember the kind of watch my husband snaps on his wrist each morning. *That's* how little contact we have."

Ethan glanced at his own bag. He hadn't even considered the possibility that his wife might already own the expensive wallet he had originally chosen. In a brief moment of what he *hoped* was brilliance, he'd returned the wallet and headed to the jewelry department instead.

"My wife and I have a beautiful home in a gated community, filled with priceless works of art that I never look at because I just don't care. Money was never important to me, but we had . . . expectations placed upon us. Today, there isn't a piece of fabric in my closet that doesn't have a designer label, and I drive an imported sports car that costs more than most people make in four years. And I don't care. I never cared about any of that. All I want is my wife back."

During the conversation, their bodies had drifted just a little closer. The man's proximity was making Melanie's pulse race.

"What makes you stay?" Ethan asked gently. "Why not leave him? He deserves it."

"I love my husband. That has never changed."

"*Something* changed."

A tear slipped down her cheek as they gazed into each other's eyes. She hated him for making her talk about this. Why now? Why tonight? While they were trapped in an elevator on Christmas Eve? She had spent so many months trying to forget. To block the images and sounds and emotions from that one night that had changed their lives forever.

"I lost our baby," she whispered through her tears. "How could he ever forgive me for that?"

An anguished Ethan closed his eyes. "And you think he blames you?"

"I *know* he blames me. Why wouldn't he? And now he's stuck in a marriage with a woman who can never give him a biological child."

"Maybe he blames himself," Ethan said, his voice shaking with emotion. "Maybe he thinks he should have taken better care of you. If he'd worked a little less and loved you a little more. Maybe if he'd read the stupid baby books . . ."

Quiet sobs wracked her body as she recalled that night. The cramps. The blood. The mad rush to the emergency room. The confirmation from the doctor that their baby was gone, and there was no chance for another.

Melanie wept uncontrollably as Ethan pulled her into his lap. She wrapped her arms around his neck and clung to him.

"I'm sorry, sweetheart," he murmured against her hair. "I love you. I never stopped loving you. Not for a minute."

She melted against him as he held her tight. She'd missed the warmth of his arms. How long had it been since he'd held her this way? How long since he'd touched her at all?

Ethan trailed his hand soothingly along her spine. He'd missed her sweet smell and the way her body fit perfectly in his arms.

He had missed his wife.

After the miscarriage, he'd had no idea how to comfort her. No idea how to deal with the mood swings and bitterness and the absolute refusal to talk about whatever she was feeling. Anything he said had been wrong, and every suggestion he made was met with resistance. It had taken Melanie's mother to convince her to see a grief counselor, and that had helped some, but the damage to their marriage was done. Because his home was in shambles, he had devoted his life to his father's company, neglecting his wife for far too long. Ethan knew that Melanie had felt responsible for the miscarriage—despite Dr. Lange's explanation that she wasn't to blame—but it never occurred to Ethan that she needed the real reassurance to come from her husband.

Ethan placed both hands along her cheeks and gently tilted her face toward his.

"It wasn't your fault," he said softly.

Melanie's eyes filled with fresh tears.

"It wasn't your fault, sweetheart. I never blamed you. Not once. I love you, and it wasn't your fault. It wasn't your fault."

She sniffled as he tenderly placed kisses along her wet cheeks, whispering over and over again that he loved her, and that she wasn't to blame. There were plenty of kids in the world who needed a good home, and they would adopt a dozen if she wanted them. He told her they would sell the house that neither of them loved, and he would build her a new one.

"In the country?"

Ethan smiled through his own tears. She had always wanted to live in the mountains, but the daily commute to his dad's firm had made the idea impossible.

Impossible, until now.

"Anywhere you want," he promised her.

With the emergency lights of the elevator shining overhead, the two of them stared into each other's eyes. They hugged tightly, wiped away each other's tears, and whispered sweetly. There was so much to say, and for the first time in months, they finally said all the important things. They had missed each other. They loved each other. And nothing was more important than rebuilding their marriage.

"How long has it been since you've been properly kissed by your husband?"

Her answer was immediate.

"New Year's Eve."

He frowned. "Surely we've kissed since last January."

"You said *properly* kissed," Melanie reminded him. "Not a photo-op peck on the lips. The last real, toe-curling kiss that made my blood boil was New Year's Eve. We were at the Hanson's holiday party, and—"

Suddenly, Ethan's mouth was on hers. Melanie groaned and slipped her hands around his neck as he deepened the kiss. Her fingers entwined in his hair, and she tugged a little, making him moan. The months of pent-up frustration and grief slipped away as their hungry kisses gave way to something softer and sweeter, until finally, Ethan buried his face against her neck. They held onto each other as they trembled with relief.

"I missed your kisses."

Melanie sighed. "I missed yours, too."

He grinned. "So, my beautiful wife, was that a *proper* kiss?"

She giggled, and the sound rocked him to his core. How long had it been since she'd laughed?

"*Im*proper, I think."

"I think so, too," Ethan agreed with a nod. "And I think these improper activities need to continue once we're home."

Melanie blushed, and he couldn't resist trailing his fingertip across her crimson cheek.

"If we ever get out of here," he grumbled.

"I can't be upset about getting stuck in this elevator," Melanie said. "We must have a Christmas angel somewhere. I mean, really, what are the odds that the two of us would be shopping in the same department store on Christmas Eve?"

Ethan couldn't argue with that. There was definitely some Christmas magic happening in this elevator.

"Speaking of which," Ethan said, nodding at the red and silver gift bag. "Did you really buy me a ten-thousand dollar watch?"

Melanie frowned. "Yes, and it's ridiculous."

Ethan laughed and lifted his hand. Snapped to his wrist was a beautiful gold watch.

Melanie sighed with relief. "It's not the same."

"We'll return it, anyway. Nobody needs a designer watch."

"Or an imported car."

"Or a Chanel wallet."

Melanie's eyes widened a little. "Did you buy me a Chanel wallet?"

"I thought about it, but I decided to do something a little different. Something symbolic."

Ethan offered her the gift bag. She excitedly reached inside and pulled out the small white box. It fit perfectly in the palm of her hand.

"Open it," he said softly.

Melanie lifted the top, and nestled inside was a necklace. Dangling from the chain was a silver mistletoe charm.

"Turn," Ethan murmured.

Melanie twisted around in his lap, and he fastened the necklace around her neck.

"It's so pretty, Ethan."

"I've missed my wife, and I wanted to guarantee that she'd let me kiss her this Christmas, so I needed mistletoe. I couldn't decide between this and the diamond earrings, but the man behind the counter insisted on the necklace."

Melanie gingerly touched the dainty charm before turning back around.

"I love it."

"I love you, Melanie."

"I love you, too." Leaning in, she kissed him tenderly. "There. Just so you can go back to the store and tell the man behind the counter that the mistletoe worked its magic."

When the lights flickered back to life and they finally made their way to the first floor, Ethan took his wife's hand and led her out of the elevator. Tonight, they would go home and begin rebuilding their marriage. They would spend Christmas Day with their families, and for the first time in months, they wouldn't have to force a smile.

And on the day after Christmas, Ethan would return the watch. He would thank the man behind the counter—a friendly manager by the name of Nick—and tell him that the mistletoe did indeed work its magic, just as he promised it would.

The Little Drummer Boy

"Justin, can you believe this snow?"

I glance up from my laptop and turn toward the office window. There's a good six inches on the sidewalk.

"When did that happen?"

"That happened, little brother, while your head was buried in that brief. And more is on the way. They say we could have close to a foot by daybreak."

It's impossible to ignore the excitement in his voice. Paul loves snow. It's just one of the reasons he refuses to leave Minneapolis. After our dad retired and handed the reins to us, I'd suggested relocating the family law firm to a sunnier climate.

But Paul won't discuss it.

Neither will my wife.

"You're thinking about that pretty wife of yours, aren't you?"

I grin. "How'd you know?"

"Because you always get this stupid smile on your face whenever you're thinking about her. You know, you make life hard for the rest of us. Haley is always asking me why I don't look at her the way you look at Megan."

"Whatever. You're crazy about your wife."

"Of course I am. She looks like a runway model and has a PhD in Microbiology. What's not to love? I just don't wear it on my sleeve like you do."

I toss some files into my briefcase. "You know, maybe you should. Women like to know they're loved."

"Yeah, yeah, you get that crap from Dad. All Mom has to do is bat those eyelashes."

It's true. After nearly forty years of marriage, our parents are still crazy about each other.

Rising from my chair, I reach for my coat and quickly zip it up. "Well, I'm out of here. I have to do some shopping."

"Shopping? On Christmas Eve?"

I shrug and grab my briefcase.

"Still haven't found her a gift, huh?"

His laughter rings down the hallway as I make my way through the lobby and out into the frosty Minneapolis air.

I hate shopping. I especially hate Christmas shopping. Megan hates shopping in general but loves Christmas, so she's happy to fight the crowds to find the perfect gifts for our family. She even loves to wrap them—even though I've repeatedly explained there are store employees who will happily do that for her. Of course, I've also tried to convince her there are decorators who can trim trees and caterers who can bake pies, but she insists on doing everything on her own.

It's just another example of how differently we were raised.

My parents freely admit we were spoiled. Dad's law firm was, and still is, one of the most respected and successful family-owned firms in the nation. Because of that success, my siblings and I never really had to struggle for a lot growing up. Mom has always been a disaster in the kitchen, so paying complete strangers to decorate the house or fix appetizers for a dinner party had been a normal part of our childhood.

Then, I met Megan Lambert —a beautiful, green-eyed, redhead who sat next to me in my third-year Legal Writing class. While the rest of us typed lecture notes on our laptops, Megan relied on pen and paper. As the daughter of a firefighter, Megan had learned from an early age how to be self-sufficient and frugal. Growing up in a single-parent home without the luxuries of . . . well, almost anything, had given her a shrewd mind and a dogged determination. She was intelligent and funny, and falling in love with her had been effortless.

By some miracle, she fell in love with me, too.

Dating had been tricky because she always refused to let me pay for anything. Popcorn at the movies. Hot dogs at the football game. It was a fight every time I reached for my wallet. It took nearly six months of dating before she finally let me pay for dinner. Despite our differences, we were absolutely crazy about each other. She taught me the importance of saving money for the future while I convinced her it was okay, within reason, to enjoy the fruits of your labor.

It was an education for both of us.

We dated for two years. After we graduated and found jobs—me with the family practice and Megan with a downtown firm specializing in real estate law—I decided there was nothing I wanted more than to ask her to be my wife.

But even that had taken some negotiating.

The first time I proposed, Megan threw the five-carat wedding ring at my head and told me to get a grip on reality.

Mom still laughs about that one.

To this day, I'm not satisfied with the modest stone that has rested on her hand for the past three years, but she loves it, and I love her, so I deal.

I tighten my scarf around my neck and continue down the icy sidewalk. While my wife loves to shop for everyone else, she isn't as forthcoming when it comes to her own Christmas list, which usually translates to me buying something outrageously expensive she forces me to return the very next day.

But it's Christmas Eve, and I am officially out of time.

Desperate for a sign, I scan the brightly-lit windows hoping inspiration will strike. Everything is twinkling and beautiful, but there's nothing hanging in the windows that she'll love.

I stop when a bookstore window catches my eye. There on display is a set of children's books. With a deep sigh, I slowly scan the titles, recognizing many of them from the bookshelf in our nursery. Back in June, we had been ecstatic to learn that we were pregnant, and the very first thing we bought was a bookshelf. Megan is thrifty with everything except books, and she had filled the bookcase with hundreds of children's stories.

Then we miscarried, and the nursery and all the books inside it remain untouched to this day.

There's only one thing in the world Megan truly wants. The one thing money can't buy.

A little me.

A little her.

A little us.

The doctor's explanation of "sometimes these things just happen" didn't satisfy either of us, but the fear of losing a baby is still so raw and suffocating that Megan won't even discuss trying again. The doctor gave us the green light, but it's now six months later and she still isn't willing to try.

I really want to try.

I pull my jacket closer and make my away around the corner to find a tiny crowd gathered just outside the coffee shop. A guitar player and carolers sing "Silent Night," and when the song ends, the little audience erupts in applause. Some of the spectators drop money into the open guitar case on the sidewalk. I'm just reaching for my wallet when someone grabs my arm.

"Do you hear drums?"

I turn and find myself face-to-face with a man. Homeless, I assume from his appearance. He's dressed in a tattered coat and looks desperately in need of a bath. I try not to cringe as he tugs on my designer suit.

"The drums," he says again, his voice forceful. "Do you hear them?"

Drums? All I see is a guitar player.

"No. Sorry. I don't hear a drum."

I turn to walk away when he tightens his grip on my arm.

"Listen, son. Just listen."

Sighing tiredly, I play along and pretend to listen. The city is deafening on any given night, but especially so on Christmas Eve. The city is filled with noise. Busy shoppers. Impatient drivers. People yelling. Horns honking.

Still, I listen. And that's when I hear it.

Rum pum pum pum.

It's faint, but it's there. A quiet, rhythmic beat that blends into the night. How this old man heard the sound is beyond me.

"You hear it, don't you?"

With a nod, I look around, hoping to find the source of the sound. The man points toward the coffee shop's covered alleyway.

"Back there," he says.

The carolers begin their rendition of "O Holy Night," and once again, I hear the "rum pum pum pum" coming from the darkness.

Intrigued, I step away from the old man and walk slowly toward the alley. Each step brings me closer to the beat, until finally, I see a little boy, nestled in the corner. His only light comes from a lantern, and a snare drum rests in his lap. The drum is scarred and the strap is frayed, but it's obviously his most prized possession.

Probably his only possession.

Does he live here? In this filthy alley? And where are his parents?

"Shall I play for you?"

His voice is just a whisper. His clothes are dirty and ragged, and the faded blue jacket he wears is about three sizes too big.

"I heard you playing," I tell him, keeping my voice soft and light. The last thing I want to do is scare the kid. "You're very good. Are you alone?"

He nods.

"Where are your parents?"

His face contorts in pain, and my stomach lurches. He can't be more than five years old. Maybe six.

"Shall I play for you?" he asks again. A little stronger this time. A little more determined.

Because I don't know what else to do, I nod. The covered alleyway has thankfully kept most of the snow away, so I find a flattened section of shredded cardboard and sit down. I don't think about the fact that I'm probably ruining my thousand-dollar suit. I just sit and listen.

The boy's sticks pound the head of the drum.

Rum pum pum pum.

Rum pum pum pum.

Each rhythmic thump pierces my soul, and when he comes to the end of his song, I reach inside my jacket for my wallet.

"No, sir," he says softly. "I don't need your money."

It's hard not to laugh. The kid is surrounded by dumpsters and living in a cardboard box. If anyone needs my money, it's this child.

"What *do* you need?"

"Just food."

"I can pay you with food?"

The boy nods vigorously, and I notice his eyes are suddenly a little brighter. The poor guy is probably starving and could definitely use a bath. Dirt cakes his face, but he has the biggest, bluest eyes I've ever seen.

"Why don't you come home with me?" I hear myself say. "My wife loves to cook."

He shakes his head. "I can't leave. My mom told me to stay here. I have to stay here."

"How old are you?"

"I'm six, sir."

"Do you have a name?"

"My name's Luke."

"Well, Luke, my name is Justin Banks, and it's cold out here. It's going to keep snowing."

"Yes, sir," he whispers, his voice trembling.

"I could take you home with me for a little while. You could take a bath and eat some dinner with us."

At the mention of a bath, he smiles.

"And then we can try to find your mom and dad."

The little boy bows his head, and when he looks up at me again, the light in his eyes is long gone.

"My mom told me to stay here."

I close my eyes in frustration. I can talk a judge and jury into almost anything. Have I really met my match in a six-year-old living in a cardboard box?

Maybe so.

But I have a secret weapon.

"You realize it is ten degrees *and* Christmas Eve? Do you know how hard it was to find a cab? This better be one delicious cup of coffee."

With a grin, I kiss my wife's cold cheek.

"Can the coffee wait just a bit? I want to introduce you to someone."

Taking her gloved hand, I gently pull her toward the alley. Understandably, she hesitates when she notices the direction in which we were headed.

"Justin, have you lost your mind?"

"Probably," I mutter, but I pull her along anyway.

With the distant light of the lantern as our guide, we slowly walk toward Luke's cardboard box. He's still there, holding his drum. His eyes grow wide when he sees the beautiful girl by my side.

"Luke, this is my wife. Her name is Megan."

Megan's eyes are frozen on the little boy. Her hand clutches mine, and I hold my breath as she examines his surroundings. There really isn't a lot to see in the dark, but you don't have to see much to know the situation isn't ideal.

"Hi, Luke."

"You're pretty," he says softly.

I smile. *Secret weapon, indeed.*

"Thank you."

"Shall I play for you?"

Megan's eyes settle on the drum strapped around his tiny body, and she nods. The drumsticks begin their slow tapping, and I wrap my arms around her, pulling her close to shield her from the snow and wind.

"Where are his parents?" she asks quietly.

"I don't know."

"We have to do something. We can't just leave him here."

"I know, sweetheart. I tried to get him to come home with us, but he just keeps saying he has to wait for his mom and dad."

"How long has he been waiting?"

"I don't know."

There's something really beautiful about my wife, and it is a quality that a lot of people never have the chance to witness. There is a certain look in her eyes and a particular expression on her face that lets you know she's made a decision, and you're an idiot if you even try to stand in her way. I have seen her work her magic on stubborn clients, deadbeat dads, and arrogant attorneys.

This kid doesn't stand a chance.

Megan drops to her knees in front of the little boy, right there on the dirty ground.

"Luke, I just made some homemade chili. Do you like chili?"

He nods quickly.

"I also made peanut butter and jelly sandwiches. Justin loves them, and I always make a bunch extra. Do you like peanut butter and jelly?"

Luke licks his lips, and my heart breaks.

"Why don't you come home with us? You can help Justin eat his sandwiches, and later, we'll try to find your parents."

I can see the indecision on his little face. He doesn't want to say no. That's another incredible thing about my wife. Telling her no is virtually impossible.

"My mom told me to stay here."

"But it's so cold, Luke," Megan murmurs, her voice breaking with emotion.

"I'll be okay."

Megan lowers her head, and for just a second, I worry that even my amazing wife has met her match. But then I hear her quiet sniffles, and Luke's face falls when he realizes she's crying.

He steps closer to her. "Why are you crying, Megan?"

She lifts her head and gazes into the little boy's eyes.

"Because I'm going to worry about you tonight. I'm afraid you'll be hungry and cold."

"Please don't cry."

I hold my breath as he reaches for her, pressing his dirty little hand against her face. Megan doesn't even flinch.

"I'll go home with you, Megan. Please don't cry." Luke then looks up at me. "Can I bring my drum?"

"Of course you can."

Megan sighs with relief and rises to her feet. With a smile as bright as the stars, the little boy takes my wife's hand. She takes mine, and the three of us walk out of the cold alleyway.

After devouring a big bowl of chili and a peanut butter sandwich, Luke is now freshly bathed and wrapped in a terrycloth robe. His head rests in Megan's lap while she reads to him from a book of fairytales as they sit in the front of the fire.

I don't ask where she found the storybook.

I don't have to.

Mesmerized, I sit across the room and watch as her fingers fluff his hair. The dirt and grime had given way to a head full of shocking blonde hair. His eyes are closed but his smile is bright as he listens to Megan's gentle voice. The Christmas tree glows in the corner of the room, and if I live to be a hundred years old, I will never forget the look on Luke's face when he first laid eyes on our tree. To me, it's just an ordinary tree. Beautiful, definitely, but just a regular tree. I've seen a thousand of them in my lifetime. But to that little boy, it was like seeing the sun for the first time. He hadn't taken his eyes off it throughout dinner, prompting Megan to finally place everything on trays and carry them into the living room so we could sit around the tree while we ate. After dinner, Megan had helped him take the longest bubble bath in the history of the world while I made some calls. The first was to my sister, Mackensey, who is the retail manager of one of the children's department stores in town. The next call was to David, my friend and an investigator with the Minneapolis PD.

Only one of those calls had proven successful.

Mackensey had arrived an hour later with enough clothes to dress a pint-sized army. David, however, was a complete dead-end.

"I can hand him over to Child Protective Services," he'd told me.

"Which means what?"

"Which means he'll likely end up as a ward of the state. They'll probably send him to a group home."

Not the answer I wanted to hear. When I had told Megan, she'd leveled me with a look that assured me that sending Luke to a group home wasn't an option at all.

I hadn't expected it to be.

A million questions race through my mind as Megan continues to read aloud to the little boy in her lap.

Where are his parents? Are they even alive? How long has he been living in that alley? What about the lantern? How is it still working? Had he been eating, and if so, what?

I shudder when I think about the dumpsters in the alley.

There is also the mystery of the drum. Convincing him to let go of the instrument long enough to take a bath had required some fancy negotiating, but my wife is an amazing woman. She had tempted the little boy with the promise of bubbles . . . which would be fun for him but bad for the drum.

I want to fumigate that drum.

Burning it would be better.

Megan suddenly falls silent, and that's when I hear Luke's quiet snores. His face is sweet and content as he snoozes in her lap. Her fingers continue to ruffle his hair, and the smile on her face as she gazes down at the little boy assures me that I have finally found the perfect Christmas gift for my wife.

And I have a feeling I won't be returning this one.

"Can you imagine what he's been through?" Megan whispers.

We're lying on the bed in the guest room with Luke sandwiched between us, still snoring peacefully.

"No, baby, I can't. I don't want to."

Her eyes brim with tears. "Tomorrow is Christmas Day. Kids all over the world will be waking up to trees surrounded by toys. If you hadn't found him, this little boy would have woken up in a cold alley without anything but a drum and a lantern."

She dissolves into quiet tears, and I reach across the sleeping boy, cradling her face in the palm of my hand.

Megan offers me a watery smile and sighs softly.

"Justin, can we keep him?"

I'm not at all surprised by the question.

"Meg, we don't know the first thing about him."

"I know."

"His parents could be out there somewhere. He could be sick."

"I know that, too."

"We'll have to go through the proper channels, starting with David and child services. This might not be easy, sweetheart."

"I understand all that. I really do."

"But?"

Megan sighs softly. "But we can't take him back to that cardboard box. I won't do that. Not ever."

"No, we won't do that, I promise. There's nothing we can do tonight. There probably isn't much we can do tomorrow since it's Christmas. But I'll call David and see what needs to be done."

She sniffles quietly, and I let my fingers linger across her moist cheek.

"I'll call Haley and get the number of the kids' pediatrician," she says. "Maybe we can convince the doctor to make a holiday house call."

And that's when it hits me. While Luke will no doubt love the new clothes that my sister had delivered, shouldn't he have . . . toys? Something fun to open on Christmas morning?

"I need to call Mack. Again."

Megan frowns. "Why?"

"I mean, I guess we could gift wrap the blue jeans, but . . ."

Megan's eyes widen. "We need toys! I didn't even think about Christmas gifts! I was more concerned with getting him out of those filthy clothes. I didn't even think . . ."

"Shh, I know. I'll take care of everything."

Her beautiful green eyes glisten. "You will?"

"Of course I will."

Carefully and slowly, I climb out of the bed. I lean down and kiss my wife before pulling the blanket around the two of them. Luke shifts in his sleep, and his blonde head finds a home against her chest.

Megan sighs contently, and I swallow the lump that has suddenly formed in my throat.

"Mackensey, you don't know how much I appreciate this."

My sister smiles as she hands me the credit card receipt. "Yes, I do. Your appreciation comes to just under $2000. Our store, and my commission, thanks you."

I grin. "Don't lie. You enjoyed yourself."

"My brother hands me his platinum card, points me toward the toy department, and tells me to go nuts. Yes, I enjoyed myself immensely." She glances at the mound of toys and frowns. "How are you going to get them wrapped?"

"Umm . . . don't you have employees who will do that for me?"

Mackensey snorts. "It's ten o'clock on Christmas Eve. My employees are at home. With their families. Which is where I should be."

I tiredly rub my face.

"But you are my brother, and you're doing a good thing here, so I'm happy to help. I can call some guys and get this stuff delivered, but I can't hire gift-wrappers for you. You'll have to figure that out on your own."

"I really appreciate this, Mack."

Mackensey reaches for the giant teddy bear. "I don't know how you'll wrap this fella, but good luck with that."

I glance at the drum set. It's red and white. Most importantly, it's clean.

"Maybe I don't have to wrap anything. Maybe just having the presents waiting under the tree will be surprise enough."

Mackensey shoots me a disapproving glare. "You can tie a big bow around the bear, but everything else needs to be wrapped! That's part of the excitement! The brightly-wrapped gifts and the mess to clean up afterwards. It's all part of the Christmas morning experience."

I have no idea what Luke's normal Christmas experience is like. Will this be his first?

If so, it was going to be one he will never forget.

"Well, little sister, I suggest you get our brother on the phone and call our parents. Tell them there is a gift wrapping party going on at my house, and I expect everyone to bring their own gift wrap and tape."

Mackensey's eyes soften. "You're really attached to this little boy, aren't you?"

"He just . . ." my voice falters as I try to wrap my mind around the situation. "He has nothing, Mackensey. I can't imagine his parents would just *leave* him, you know? He's living in a cardboard box in the alley, and his only possessions are a lantern and a drum. He devoured Megan's chili as if he'd never seen food in his life, and then I watched as she bathed him in a tub full of bubbles. Right now, he's wrapped in her arms and sleeping like a baby. So, yes, you could say that we've become attached."

Mackensey walks around the counter and wraps her arms around my middle, squeezing tightly.

"We'll make Christmas perfect for him," she says.

The delivery guys arrive just after midnight. They don't seem happy, but I tip them outrageously, which seems to brighten their moods a little.

Now to get it all wrapped.

Paul, Haley, and my nieces were on their way over, as were my parents and Mackensey. After calling and giving them strict instructions to *not* ring the doorbell, I peek into the guest room to find Megan and Luke still fast asleep.

Should I let her sleep?

Megan loves to wrap gifts. It's an obsession, really, and I have a feeling she'll kill me if she doesn't get a chance at this mound of toys.

I slowly walk over to her side of the bed and kneel onto the floor. It takes several soft kisses against her forehead before she begins to stir.

"Justin?"

"Hi, sweetheart."

"What time is it?"

"It's pretty late, but I want to show you something."

Through sleepy eyes, Megan glances down at the sleeping boy in her arms.

"He's been restless. Bad dreams, I think."

With a life like his, I can only assume nightmares are common.

"We'll keep the door open," I tell her.

With a nod, Megan gently slides Luke out of her arms and wraps the blanket tightly around him before following me out into the hallway.

I'm a little nervous about this reveal. My wife and sister are the very best of friends, but Megan is rarely happy when I hand Mack my credit card. Mackensey likes to shop, and she's good at it, but she has our mother's expensive taste, which clashes with Megan's idea of casual comfort.

"Okay, don't get mad," I tell her.

"Why would I—"

Megan's eyes grow wide when we enter the living room. We might as well have walked right into a toy store. Every flat surface is covered with some type of toy. The giant teddy bear is nestled close to the tree. The drum set is perched right next to the bright blue electric car. There's a red bicycle with training wheels and the deluxe train set that surrounds the tree. We have Legos, action figures, and a gaming system with enough video games to last until he's a teenager. Mackensey, in her brilliance, didn't just buy toys, however. There are more clothes, shoes, bedding, and enough books to open a library.

The room is filled with literally anything and everything a child could ever want on Christmas morning.

Megan has yet to say a word.

"I know it's a lot, Meg, and I know we're probably going to argue, but . . . I just wanted him to have a perfect Christmas day. It might be his first. We don't know. And I just wanted to make it special for him."

With tears sparkling in her eyes, she wraps her arms around my neck.

"Thank you, Justin. Thank you for making it perfect."

I breathe a sigh of relief. "Now we just have to get it all wrapped."

Her face turns ashen, and I laugh.

"Don't worry. I've called in reinforcements."

It's nearly dawn by the time my family heads home. Luke hasn't stirred, even with the commotion of our family as we wrapped gifts and placed them under the tree. They all promised to be back later so they can meet the little boy who has completely stolen our hearts.

"A Mercedes-Benz?" Megan smirks at me as I finish tying the bright red bow around the hood of the toy car. "What? Was the Porsche sold out?"

"As a matter of fact, yes."

She smiles brightly, and I can't recall the last time I've seen my wife this unbelievably happy.

Exhausted, but happy.

"Come here."

I take her hand and pull her toward the couch. She snuggles close as the two of us admire our handiwork. The gifts are bright and beautiful as they encircle the giant Christmas tree. What I once thought was just an ordinary tree is now something . . . more. Something beautiful. And it has nothing to do with the gifts beneath its branches. It's beautiful because it symbolizes so much.

Hope. Love. Family.

What more could any little boy—or any grown-up, for that matter—

want on Christmas morning?

"You know, I've heard a drum set is the leading cause of divorce."

I wink at my wife. "You'd never leave me."

Megan's face softens, and she snuggles deeper into my arms. "True. Why would I? You've given me the world, and I don't think I've ever truly appreciated it until now."

"It's just a bunch of toys, Meg."

"Not to Luke, it isn't. It's been an amazing day, and *you* made that happen. Look at him."

I smile and watch as Luke examines his new drum. Of course, out of all the toys under the tree, it's his favorite.

I have felt true happiness twice in my life. The first was on my wedding day. The second was the day we found out we were pregnant. Today, I have a third moment to add to the list.

The absolute joy on Luke's face as he tiptoed into the living room.

"For me?"

With every rip of the wrapping paper, he had uttered those words, and more than once, I had caught my mother wiping away her own tears. Our family fell in love with him, and I know that nothing under any of our trees could be better than the gift we had given each other today.

Joy through the eyes of a child.

We had given him that.

We had given that to each other.

The day had been a whirlwind. Megan and my mom prepared a gigantic breakfast, and my family had gathered around our living room floor while we ate. Luke would take a few bites, then jump up and play for a while before returning to his plate. Even I could sense that it was probably sensory overload for the kid, and no one was surprised when he started complaining with a tummy ache. My sister-in-law, Haley, simply grabbed her cell, dialed the number to her pediatrician, and within an hour, he was making a house call on Christmas Day.

There are definite perks to being in the Banks family.

The initial diagnosis was simple indigestion—too much food on a sensitive stomach that probably hadn't seen a decent meal in ages. Still, we made an appointment for the next day to give Luke a complete physical exam. I listened with pride as my wife went into full Mama Bear mode, asking a million questions that I never would have even considered.

It's just one of the many reasons why I love her.

Now we're alone, with just the rhythmic sound of his new drum echoing in our ears. Admittedly, the drum *is* a little loud, but we don't mind. Luke's happiness is worth any headache.

"You really took care of everything."

I kiss the top of her hair. "I told you I would. As long as I'm breathing, you'll never want for anything, and neither will our children—biological or otherwise."

Megan tilts her face toward mine. A single tear streaks down her cheek, and I gently wipe it away.

"You have my permission to spoil them rotten."

I smile and kiss her gently.

The next day is blustery and cold as we drive to the pediatrician's office. His building is close to Luke's alleyway, and Megan and I both see the fear in the little boy's eyes as he watches it pass just outside the tinted windows.

"I need my lantern," Luke whispers from the back seat, his voice filled with fear.

"Why do you need your lantern, sweetheart?" Megan asks.

"What if it gets dark again? What if it gets cold again?"

I tighten my grip on the steering wheel and try to hide how much his words break my heart. Megan—always a hundred times stronger than I could ever hope to be—just whispers her promise that he will never be cold again.

Once Megan and Luke are inside and registered with the receptionist, I decide to go back to the alley to grab that old lantern and look for any clues that might have been hidden in the darkness.

It looks even worse in the daylight.

The filth is the least of it. Rats scurry from the dumpster as I walk toward the cardboard box that's now covered with snow.

The wind must have blown it in. If I hadn't found him . . .

"I bet you're looking for this," a voice echoes behind me.

I turn to find myself face-to-face with the old homeless man. He's still wearing the same clothes from the night we met, and he's holding Luke's lantern.

"Sir, I can't thank you enough. I never would have followed the sound of the drum if you hadn't brought it to my attention."

"*Sir.* It's been a long time since anyone's called me that." He lets out a chuckle and nods. "Little Luke beats on that drum every night, and no one notices. It's amazing what we can hear if we just take a moment and really listen."

"How long has he been living here?"

"A few weeks. Three days ago, his parents went to get food, and they never came back."

Bile rises in my throat.

"They were good people and loved their son very much," the man says, noticing the rage on my face. "I'm sure it wasn't by choice that they didn't return."

Suddenly, I'm even angrier at the man standing before me. "You knew he was living back here! You knew he was cold and alone, and you did nothing?"

He looks at me quizzically. "What could I have done?"

"You could have taken him to a hospital! To a shelter. To the police. You should have gotten him some help!"

The old man's smiles sadly. "I'm sure you've called the police, and I'm sure they told you what happens to homeless kids and orphans."

My blood runs cold. *Group home.*

"Still, that would have been better than letting him freeze to death!"

"The lantern kept him warm."

"Lanterns run out of oil, eventually."

"Some do, yes."

I angrily rip the lantern out of his hand. "He's just a little boy, and you should have helped him."

The old man smiles, but this time, his face is peaceful.

"I did help him," he says quietly. "Granted, it took some time. I didn't think you were ever going to leave your office. The snow helped."

My eyes narrow. *Was the old man a stalker?*

"I *did* help him," the man whispers, placing his hand against my shoulder. "And I helped *you.* Merry Christmas, Justin."

A gust of icy wind blows across my face, and I close my eyes to shield them from the cold.

When I open them again, the old man is gone.

One year later

"Shall I play for you?" Luke asks me. His smile is bright and his eyes are clear and happy as he sits down at the piano.

It's amazing the difference a year can make.

It's Christmas Eve, and our family dinner party is in full swing. Megan and Luke spent the day baking cookies and pies. For the first time, she allowed me to call a caterer for everything else. Juggling motherhood with her job at the law firm had been an adjustment for Megan, but the happiness that glowed from her beautiful green eyes assured me that she wouldn't want it any other way.

It had taken several heartbreaking months and endless mounds of paperwork, but this Christmas, Luke is officially our son.

As we had feared, his parents had succumbed to the harsh winter, and their bodies had been identified one week later at the county hospital. The only other family we found was a cousin in St. Paul—a mother of five who made it clear that the last thing she needed was another mouth to feed.

After that, the paperwork had moved right along.

Luke's fingers sail seamlessly along the keys of the grand piano, filling the air with the sounds of Christmas. We had finally convinced him expand his musical horizons for something a little less deafening, and he had taken to the piano like a fish to water.

Our son is amazing.

He is now seven years old and in the second grade. We had considered having him repeat first grade, but his teachers felt that, with a little encouragement over the summer, he would be more than ready to keep up with his second grade classmates. Megan had taken a leave of absence from the firm in order to work with him, and by the time school began in September, our son had been doing multiplication—a skill his classmates wouldn't be learning until later in the year.

Needless to say, Luke is now a little bored at school.

He has piano lessons twice a week and karate lessons with his Uncle Paul every Friday night. He is well-adjusted, healthy, and happy, and the absolute joy of our lives.

The nursery had been quickly converted into a "big boy's room," and the books which had lined the shelves for so long are now read each and every night. Sitting on top of his dresser is the lantern and his old snare drum.

He couldn't bear to part with them.

Neither could we.

So much has changed, and I can't imagine life can get much better.

And then it does—with one last Christmas gift from my wife.

"I didn't see this under the tree." I grin as she hands me a small package.

It's late on Christmas Eve, and our family has finally headed home. Luke is asleep in his room, and Megan and I are getting ready to arrange the gifts from Santa around the Christmas tree.

"I know," Megan says. "I didn't want you to open it in front of everyone else."

Intrigued, I raise the box close to my ear and shake it gently.

It rattles.

Interesting.

"Just open it," Megan whispers, her eyes filled with tears.

Very carefully, I pull the ribbon and lift the lid. Nestled inside the gift tissue is a shiny, silver rattle.

I look at her with wide eyes as tears stream down her face.

"Merry Christmas, Daddy."

Words fail me, but none are really needed. I just lift her into my arms and hold her close.

Suddenly, the unmistakable sound of sleigh bells can be heard in the distance.

Megan gasps. "Is that . . .?"

I remember the words of the old man who has truly given me everything I've ever wanted, and I smile.

"It's amazing what we can hear if we just take a moment and really listen," I whisper.

About the Author

Amazon bestselling author Sydney Logan holds a Master's degree in Elementary Education. She is the author of three novels - *Lessons Learned, Mountain Charm, and Soldier On*. Sydney has also penned four short stories and is a contributor to *Chicken Soup for the Soul*.

A native of East Tennessee, Sydney enjoys playing piano and relaxing on her porch with her wonderful husband and their very spoiled cat.

Visit her online at www. sydneylogan.com.